Scarlet SILVER

The Vague Vagabond

Original concept by Sarah McConnell
Written by Lucy Courtenay
Illustrations by Sarah McConnell

Hodder
Children's
Books

A division of Hachette Children's Books

ISBN: 978 0 340 98917 3 (HB)
ISBN: 978 0 340 95972 5 (PB)
Printed and bound in Great Britain by Bookmarque Ltd,
Croydon, Surrey

The paper used in this book by Hodder Children's Books
is a natural recyclable product made from wood grown in
sustainable forests. The manufacturing processes conform
to the environmental regulations of the country of origin.
The hard coverboard is recycled.

Hodder Children's Books
a division of Hachette Children's Books
338 Euston Road, London NW1 3BH

Hodder Children's Books Australia
Level 17/207 Kent Street, Sydney, NSW 2000

An Hachette UK Company
www.hachette.co.uk

Contents

The Ritual

The heat pressed down on the deck of *55 Ocean Drive* like a warm, wet flannel. The breeze felt like a dog panting in your face. Fat black clouds were gathering overhead. Even the worst pirate in the world could have guessed that a thunderstorm was coming.

"Do you think a thunderstorm is coming, Scarlet?" asked Lila Silver, fixing the straps on her skull-and-crossbones bikini and staring anxiously upwards.

Scarlet Silver, pirate captain of *55 Ocean Drive*, was used to her mother's questions. This might have been the family's first pirate voyage together, but they had been at sea for several months now. "Probably, Mum," she said.

"Lightning strikes in thunderstorms," said the man with the twisty moustache standing with his arm around Lila's shoulders. "Yes, Dad," said Scarlet. "It does."

"Well," said Melvin Silver, twisting his moustache a little tighter, "don't you think Cedric should come down now?"

Scarlet gazed up at where her little brother was fixing *55 Ocean Drive*'s new lightning conductor to the top of the mainmast. "It's an important job," she said. "We can't risk being struck by lightning,

not now we're so close to finding Granny's tremendous treasure."

There was a growl of thunder. Ralph the ship's cat shot into the cabin with his fur on end. Close behind him swooped the ship's two birds, Bluebeard the budgie and Lipstick the parrot.

When the animals start hiding, you know you're in trouble, thought Scarlet. How much longer was Cedric going to take?

"Get DOWN Cedric, you daft doughnut!" roared the elderly pirate at the ship's wheel. "You'll be fried like a frog fritter!"

"You'll thank me, One-Eyed Scott," Cedric said, still tinkering.

"You'll be a toasted teabag!" One-Eyed Scott shouted. The chicken bones in his straggly hair clinked and clattered as he shook his head.

"He's right, Cedric," said the bearded old pirate sitting on the ship's railings. "You can't be too careful with lightning."

"You're one to talk, Grandpa Jack," said Scarlet, eyeing the metal fishing rod in her grandfather's hands. "Don't you think you should put that away now?"

There was a lazy flicker of lightning between two clouds close by. Scarlet made a decision. "Cedric?" she called up the mast. "As your captain, I'm ordering you to get down from there. NOW."

Cedric tightened one last screw. He tucked his tools into his tool belt. Then he hooked up the special sliding attachments

13

on the leg splints that he used to help him walk, and slid down a rope to the deck.

Lighting struck the conductor like a sledgehammer. The ship rocked. Everyone clung to the railings as the sea fizzed and steamed around them. Raindrops the size of tennis balls started bouncing around the deck.

"See?" said Cedric, pulling himself up

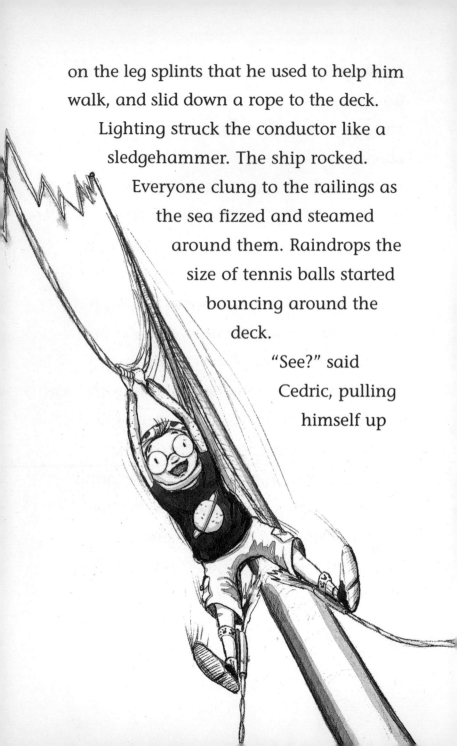

on the ship's railings. "Nothing to worry about."

Lately, the Silvers had done a lot of worrying. They'd worried about how to sail a pirate ship which, until fairly recently, they'd thought was just a boat-shaped house. They'd worried about how to get on to islands, and how to get off them. They'd worried about solving the treasure riddle that Long Joan Silver, Scarlet's granny, had taught Lipstick the parrot before she had been eaten by a giant shrimp on her tragic last voyage. And through it all, they'd worried about Gilbert Gauntlet, vile villain and owner of the shiniest frock-coat buttons on the Seven Seas, who'd fought them every step of the way.

But now they'd solved the riddle and found four puzzle pieces to clip on to Scarlet's treasure pendant – and the lightning had passed without doing anything to *55 Ocean Drive* other than smoking a row of kippers pegged out in the rigging by One-Eyed Scott – it was time to celebrate.

Lila and Melvin had been playing merry pirate tunes on their instruments ever since leaving land the previous day. The crew had been treated to the *Yo-Ho Hoedown*, *The Funky Eyepatch* and *Up on High* – all of which were impossible not to dance to. Scarlet had tried to get everyone's attention back to their treasure hunt, but had found herself dancing along with the rest of them until the thunderstorm had struck. It wasn't

every day that you foiled a villain five
times and solved a tricky riddle after all.

But it was time to Get Back to Business.
They may have found all the puzzle
pieces, but they still had to work out

what the whole thing *meant*.

Pirates like rituals, and Scarlet had planned a Grand and Final Putting-Together of the Puzzle. She made everyone sit on the deck as she hung the square pendant on the spokes of the ship's wheel. The green enamel with its wavy blue lines glinted in the sunlight.

"Underwater, overboard, up on high and wave the sword," Lipstick squawked. "Solve the riddle at your leisure, come and find tremendous treasure. Rar!"

Everyone cheered, even though they'd heard the rhyme a hundred times.

"The first Piece," Scarlet said, pulling out a piece of blue enamel with two straight edges and one wavy edge. "*Underwater*. May it bring us Luck."

She clipped the first piece to the top

corner of the pendant with a lovely magnetic *clunk*.

"The second Piece," she continued. "*Overboard*. May it bring us Courage."

"Yippee!" shouted Grandpa Jack as Scarlet clipped it into place.

"The third Piece," said Scarlet. "*Up on high*. May it help us to See Things Clearly."

"Bottoms," said Lipstick, and nipped Melvin's ear.

Scarlet took out the piece they'd only found the day before. "And lastly," she said with pride, "the fourth Piece. *Wave the sword*. May it Show Us the Way." She kissed it and clipped it on.

Everyone gazed at the pendant. There was a big, fat, heavy Question in the air. They could all feel it. So Melvin asked it.

"Um," he said, clearing his throat.
"Why d'you suppose there's a bit missing
in the middle?"

Scary Hairy Alexander Mary

"But we've *solved* the riddle," Scarlet
wailed for the hundredth time. "Four
parts. Four puzzle pieces for the pendant.
Simple ... Oh Mum, stop playing that,
will you? It's driving me *nuts*."

The tragic chords of *The Last of the
Maltesers* faltered and stopped as Lila
lowered her accordion. Ralph crept down
from the yardarm, where he'd been
hiding ever since One-Eyed Scott had

21

shouted something so rude that one of
the glass panes in the cabin door had
shattered.

"Scarlet?" said Melvin, from his
position at the ship's wheel. "According
to this chart, we're about to sail into a
big blank nothing. No one's ever filled in
what happens this far past Bottle Island.
What are we going to do?"

"Here be dragons," said Cedric, from
his post up in the crow's nest.

"Dragons?" Lila said in a quaky voice.

"It's only a quote, Mum," Cedric said.
"They put it on maps in the old days,
when they didn't know what lay ahead."

Just in case it *wasn't* only a quote,
everyone peered over the side of the ship.
They were several days from land now.
The sea stretched around them, blue and

shimmering and exactly the same in
every single direction.

Scarlet put her head in her hands. *Oh
Granny,* she thought to herself. *Why did
you have to be so cryptic? A letter would
have been so much easier. Something along
the lines of: Hello everyone, sorry I got eaten
by that giant shrimp, here's an easy-peasy
map that will take you to some tremendous
treasure, always remember to dry between*

your toes, love Granny. It's not much to ask, is it?

"Have we got another map?" Melvin asked in a hopeful voice.

"Gran left a million maps in her pirate chest," Scarlet said grumpily, swinging the four-cornered treasure pendant between her fingers. She was seriously thinking of flinging it overboard. "Take your pick."

"Hey!" Cedric yelled down from the crow's nest. "Something at twelve o'clock!"

"Lunch?" said Melvin.

"Cedric means something is straight ahead of us," Scarlet said.

"A dragon!" Lila screeched.

Everyone rushed to the side of the ship. They stared at the object on the water.

"The deadly Log Dragon," Melvin smirked. "Known for its nasty splinters."

"It's not a log," Scarlet said, as Lila whacked Melvin on the arm for teasing her. "It's a whole *bunch* of logs."

"Tootling tuna fish," said One-Eyed Scott. "'Tis a raft!"

It *was* a raft – and it was occupied. Strapped on board with a long and rather smelly-looking rope was a *person* with what looked like a seagull resting on his head.

"Ahoy there!" Scarlet shouted.

The person's salty-looking eyelids fluttered open. He gazed up at the crew of *55 Ocean Drive*. The crew of *55 Ocean Drive* gazed back.

"Are you – a mirage?" croaked the person.

"No," said Cedric. "We're a three-masted schooner."

Scarlet kicked a rope ladder over the side of the ship. The person shakily untied himself from the raft and clambered up, collapsing on *55 Ocean Drive*'s deck. He *ponged*. Lila waved her hand in front of her nose. Then, not wishing to appear rude, she quickly pretended to be swatting a fly.

Once the person had tipped a couple of buckets of seawater over himself, dragged a comb through his hair and beard and borrowed a pair of One-Eyed Scott's trousers, he told them his story.

"They calls me Scary Hairy Alexander Mary," he began.

Cedric sniggered.

"Mary?" said Lila politely. "That's an unusual name for a pirate."

"'Twas my father's name," growled Scary Hairy Alexander Mary. "The Scary Hairy part ..." He grinned unpleasantly. "Let's just say, I earned my pirate boots."

Scarlet had a feeling that the Scary Hairy part had just been added to make the Mary sound a bit more butch. But of course, it would have been rude to say as much.

"'Tis a mouthful, I know," Scary Hairy Alexander Mary continued. "So I's generally known as Sham. For short, like. Yeah."

"How long have you been shipwrecked, Mr Sham?" Melvin asked.

Sham's eyes glittered strangely. "Weeks and weeks," he said.

"But what did you *eat*?" Cedric gasped.

"Seagulls if I could catch 'em, seagull droppings if I couldn't," said Sham, slurping greedily from the flagon of rum that Grandpa Jack had given him. "Oh, 'twas terrible. *Terrible.*"

"Did you drink your own—" Cedric began with a giggle.

"*Cedric,*" Lila interrupted. "What sort of question is that? I'm sure Mr Sham did nothing of the sort."

Sham cleared his throat and concentrated on his rum.

"What happened to your ship?" asked Scarlet. She noticed that Sham's eyes had started sliding from side to side like the mercury in her mum's thermometer.

"It sank," said Sham.

"Bad smells are horrible to live with," Lila said, nodding. "I'd have abandoned ship too."

"Not stank, Mum," said Scarlet, feeling embarrassed. "Sank."

There was a nasty silence. Even two buckets of seawater hadn't entirely got rid of the smell of old fish that hung around their guest.

"Terrible business," Sham continued as Lila blushed. "Everyone drowned. Everything lost."

"Except you," Melvin pointed out.

"Aye," said Sham, looking more cheerful.

"What were you doing in these parts?" asked One-Eyed Scott.

Sham's eyes slid around rather quickly. "A terrible hard adventure, the likes of which you wouldn't never believe," he said, bringing his hands to his face.

"Oooh," said Cedric. "Did you see dragons? Or aliens, maybe?" After piracy, aliens were Cedric's favourite thing.

Sham's eyes were really whizzing now. They were mesmerising, if you looked at them for long enough. Scarlet shook her head to clear it.

"We're looking for treasure," said Lila.

Scarlet frowned. "Mum," she began.

"Hush, Scarlet," Lila said, flapping a hand in a mixed attempt to waft away the bad-fish smell and tell Scarlet to be quiet at the same time. "We're all friends here, aren't we? We're rather stuck actually, Mr Sham. We're after some tremendous treasure, you see, only we've run out of clues."

Sham's eyes stopped whizzing. They went as hard as glass. "Treasure, eh?" he said.

Cedric plucked the pendant from Scarlet's hands. Before Scarlet had time to snatch it back, he was showing it to their smelly guest.

"We've got the four corner pieces, you see," he said eagerly, "only this middle part is missing, and we don't know why ..."

Something about Sham bothered Scarlet. She reached for the pendant, but it was too late. Sham had already taken it in his hands and was gazing at it. He crooned at the pendant like it was alive.

"What a beauty you are, eh … all glimmering there … what are your secrets, my pretty?"

Sham turned the pendant over. Scarlet thought his eyes were going to pop out of his head as he pointed at the interlinked pattern of Vs that were etched all over the pendant's golden back and hissed:

"*'Tis the sign of the Vague Vagabond!*"

Here All Along

Lipstick gave a deafening screech at the mention of the Vague Vagabond.

"Oooh," said Lila in excitement. "Who's he?"

Sham leaned in close. The smell was overpowering. Scarlet shifted back.

"The Vague Vagabond is a legend," Sham whispered. "A ghost. A rumour. They say he has an island and a lagoon all to himself. No one has ever seen him, and no one knows where his island is. But all who sail in these waters know of his treasure, buried so deep and so secret that some say the Vague Vagabond himself don't know where it is no more."

The crew was spellbound by Sham's words and his weird, sliding eyes. From her position a little further back, however, Scarlet noticed Sham inching the pendant towards his own pocket.

"Hey!" she said indignantly, grabbing the pendant back. "That's not yours!"

Anger blazed across Sham's face. For someone who'd been adrift for weeks, he moved very quickly. Before the Silvers could get to their feet, Sham had taken a running leap off the side of the ship and was now swimming strongly for his raft.

"Vermin!" One-Eyed Scott yelled, shaking his fist.

"Villain! Vinaigrette!"

"He won't get far," said Melvin. "Not on that lump of—"

An outboard motor had suddenly appeared on the raft. The unmistakable sound of an engine roared into life. Before the crew's astonished eyes, Sham zoomed away in a plume of spray.

"I knew he was dodgy," said Melvin as the raft disappeared over the horizon. "You could tell."

"I didn't see you doing much about it, Dad," Scarlet pointed out.

Melvin scratched his head. "It was his eyes," he said rather sheepishly.

"I can't believe I showed him the pendant," Cedric muttered.

"I started it when I mentioned the treasure," Lila said, wringing her hands. "I don't know what came over me."

"No point crying over spilt spanners," said One-Eyed Scott. "At least we don't have to niff that pong no more. Who was that fella? He weren't shipwrecked, that's for sure."

Scarlet put her hands on her hips. "Didn't you notice?" she said.

"Notice what?" Lila asked.

"On the sole of his foot when he dived off the ship," said Scarlet. "A tattoo of a pirate fist clutching a wad of cash."

The crew gasped.

"Stinking stovepipes," said One-Eyed Scott, clapping his hands to his head.

"Gilbert Gauntlet's logo!" Grandpa Jack cried in horror.

Scarlet paced the deck, trying to think. "Looks like Gilbert Gauntlet stuck old Scary Hairy Alexander Mary out here to lie in wait for us," she said. "Or – maybe not us, exactly, but anyone heading this way. Anyone looking for the Vague Vagabond … Could *his* treasure be the same as *our* treasure?"

She gazed down at the pendant in her hand, turning it over to study the pattern of Vs on the back. They *had* to work it out. As soon as Sham reported back to his boss, Gilbert Gauntlet would be after them like a greased cannonball.

Everyone was put on riddle duty. Scarlet laid the pendant on the deck, and wrote the riddle on the mast with a piece of chalk so everyone could see it. What had they missed? They turned it upside down, back to front and inside out. They swapped the Es for the As, and the Os for the Us, and then they swapped them back again. Lipstick grew so sick of having to recite it that he flew up to the crow's nest in a sulk. Lila made hard-boiled seagull-egg sandwiches to help everyone think, but all they did was make One-Eyed Scott fart.

After two days of desperation and terrible smells, Scarlet climbed up into the rigging and dangled there, her arms folded across her chest. Hanging upside down helped her brain move quicker.

Something to do with the extra blood in her head, she decided.

She was about to swing the right way round again when she stopped and frowned down at the pendant in its usual place on the deck. From up here, it was just a smudge of blue and green.

Blue … Green …

"GALLOPING GORGONZOLAS!" Scarlet yelled. She flipped herself round and slid down the mast. "NOTHING's missing! It's all here!"

Everyone put down their seagull-egg sandwiches.

"Of course there's something missing," said Lila. "There's a great big space in the middle."

"It's not a space, Mum," said Scarlet. She snatched up the pendant and

raced for the steps,
seizing the handrail
and sliding all the way
down. Sprinting into
her cabin, she flung up
the lid of Long Joan
Silver's old pirate chest. Pirate
gadgets, maps, pants and socks
spilled on to the floor. Scarlet flung
everything left and right, burrowing
down ... down ... down ... until her hand
closed on an old roll of parchment at the
very bottom.

"It's been here all along," she said
breathlessly, as her family rushed into
the cabin and goggled at the mess. "I just
didn't see it ..."

She unfurled the parchment. Everyone
stared at the map that was revealed. It

showed a blue sea and a green island.

An island exactly the same shape as the space in the middle of the pendant.

Never Give Up

The deck of *55 Ocean Drive* was bathed in sunlight and happiness as Scarlet pinned up the map of the island where everyone could see it. The crew started whooping and dancing around the mast like it was a maypole. Lipstick swooped overhead screeching "Bottoms!" joyously every two seconds. Ralph tried to eat Bluebeard, which he only ever did when he was in a really good mood. One-Eyed Scott tried a cartwheel, but got stuck halfway and had to be helped down the other side by a madly giggling Grandpa Jack.

"If Granny's treasure isn't right here," Scarlet shouted through the cheering as she jabbed the island with one finger, "then I'm a chocolate-fudge sundae."

"I wish," Cedric grinned, riding up on Melvin's shoulders.

"Cedric, my boy," Melvin cried as he kicked his legs as high as they would go, "once we have that tremendous treasure, you can have all the chocolate-fudge sundaes in the world!"

Scarlet studied the numbers running along the bottom of the map. "If these coordinates are right," she said, "this island is about a week's sailing in that direction." She pointed east, glancing at the little printed compass in the top right-hand corner of the map.

She glanced again.

What she saw didn't make sense.

Compasses usually showed North, South, East and West, marked with the letters N, S, E and W. Some compasses went further, running the letters together in between the main compass points: North-North-East, South-South-West, so no one (except those with a truly terrible sense of direction) could possibly get lost.

The letters around the swirly-centred compass on *this* map were: L, E, A and N.

"Hornswoggling hooverbags," said One-Eyed Scott as Scarlet grabbed him by the arm and showed him. "Left, East, Around and North, maybe? We got ourselves another puzzle here, Scarlet."

Grandpa Jack, Lila, Melvin and Cedric stopped dancing. Lipstick swore loudly. Ralph let go of Bluebeard.

"My Joan always loved puzzles," said Grandpa Jack, scratching his beard. "Crosswords, griddlers, sud-hokey-cokies."

"Well, you know what?" said Scarlet crossly. "*I don't.*"

She marched through the cabin door, slammed it shut and stalked down the stairs. All these riddles were like opening one box to find another box, and another one, and another, endlessly, on and on. Where was the fun in *that*?

"Why is this so hard, Granny?" she demanded, staring at the full-length

portrait of Long Joan Silver that hung on the cabin wall. "We haven't been pirates for very long, you know. Mum's only just figured out the difference between port and starboard. Don't you think we've got enough problems already?"

Standing tall in her favourite purple velvet frock coat and thigh-length black boots, the portrait of Long Joan Silver twinkled down at Scarlet. There was a tiny smile on the pirate queen's face.

In the portrait, there were three small words carved on the blade of Long Joan's cutlass. Scarlet had always known what they said. Today, they felt like a message.

NEVER GIVE UP.

Scarlet made a decision. They would follow the coordinates and try not to worry about the weird letters on the compass. NEVER GIVE UP. If Long Joan Silver had stuck by those words, Scarlet would too.

Four days passed. Scarlet concentrated on following the coordinates, hoping the letters around the compass would make sense eventually.

Feeling their captain's mood, the crew quietly got on with their jobs. Lila served up as many interesting variations on fried fish and seagull eggs as she could think of. Melvin got so good at hoisting and lowering the mainsail that he hardly thought about what his fingers were doing any more. Cedric ate all his meals up in the crow's nest, determined to be the first one to spot land. Grandpa Jack and One-Eyed Scott modified their fishing rods and managed to land an octopus, while up in the rigging Ralph and the two birds slept as much as they possibly could.

On the fifth day, a tiny sandbank sidled on to the horizon like an apologetic pancake. Melvin dropped anchor. They waded ashore, desperate to stretch their legs after more than a week at sea. The water was so shallow that they could count the shells under their feet.

"I'm going to build a massive sandcastle," Cedric announced.

"Good idea," said Scarlet. She didn't want to point out that there was nothing else to do on a sandbank.

"Now," said Lila, unstrapping her accordion from her back. "Who's for a quick burst of *The Groovy Groat*?"

Grandpa Jack and One-Eyed Scott made a fire with some of *55 Ocean Drive*'s firewood. Soon, the air was filled with the smell of griddled octopus and the "boo boo be doo"s in *The Groovy Groat* chorus. Scarlet built a chair-shaped sandcastle and sat on it, staring out at the endless sea. Ralph curled up on her feet, and Bluebeard perched on her hat.

The sun sank and the moon rose, changing the sea to a sheet of black glass. The sandcastle chair Scarlet was sitting on turned grey. Bluebeard tucked his head underneath his small blue wing, and Lipstick did the same with his red one on Lila's shoulder. It was peaceful, and after several games of Charades and I Spy – which only lasted two rounds, sand and sea – the Silvers and One-Eyed Scott fell asleep to the gentle lull of the sloshing shore.

Only the fish heard the puttering sound of a motorised raft approaching the sandbank. Only the seagulls smelt the fishy stink and gathered curiously overhead. The moonlight sparkled on the raft's pale wake as Sham cut his engine and coasted up beside the silent *55 Ocean Drive*. He and his passenger gazed over at the sandbank, where Scarlet and her sleeping crew lay dreaming of riddles.

The tall blond passenger wore a black pirate coat that made him almost invisible in the darkness. If it hadn't been for his buttons gleaming in the moonlight, even Sham wouldn't have known Gilbert Gauntlet was sitting next to him.

The Swirly-Shaped Spinning Thingy

"Told you I'd find 'em," Sham boasted. He followed Gilbert Gauntlet up the rope ladder dangling from the side of *55 Ocean Drive*. "The Bleeping Blinker is the best homing device on the Seven Seas. I stuck it on the bottom of one of their seawater buckets, the dopes."

"Shame you weren't so clever when you tried to pocket that pendant," said Gilbert Gauntlet. His voice was cold.

Sham had thought of this. "Ah, but *is* it a shame?" he said, waving a gnarled and rather fishy finger in the air. "Ain't this all so much better, you coming here and filching it for yourself, Mr Gauntlet sir, yer honour?"

Gilbert Gauntlet stood on the deck of *55 Ocean Drive* and gazed around. "The pendant," he said. "Where is it?"

They both glanced over at the moonlit sandbank and its snoozing occupants.

"Don't tell me," said Gilbert Gauntlet through gritted teeth. "Around the girly's skinny neck."

"We don't need the pendant, sir," Sham gabbled, pointing. "There's a map, pinned to the mast! And I swears it's the same shape as what was in the middle of that trinket!"

"My dear Scary Hairy fellow," said Gilbert Gauntlet, flicking the map with the tip of a well-manicured finger. "Never assume anything where the girly is concerned."

"Ain't you gonna nick it, sir?" said Sham, watching as Gilbert Gauntlet stared at the map's strange swirly-shaped compass.

"You common sailor folk can be very stupid," said Gilbert Gauntlet. "Why would I want to 'nick' it?"

Sham wondered if this was a trick question. "Because you wants the treasure, sir?" he ventured.

"I do want the treasure, Scary Hairy Alexander Mary," Gilbert Gauntlet said. "I do indeed. I also want the girly's head on a plate with two sprigs of parsley in her ears. But it strikes me that we don't have all the information we need, and perhaps the girly does." He twiddled his finger around the strange compass. "So won't it be so much easier to let her find the treasure *for* us?" he finished.

"Genius, Mr Gauntlet sir," said Sham. He had no idea what his boss was talking about.

"I'm not saying that I want it to be easy," Gilbert Gauntlet said. "In fact, the harder the better. But with your Bleeping Stinker Blinker thing, we'll keep her in our sights, and choose our moment. I'm awfully good at swooping in at the last minute and claiming the prize for myself. It's how I got so much richer than *you*."

Sham kept nodding.

"Let's tinker around with the girly's

61

hull, shall we?" Gilbert Gauntlet
murmured. His voice rose. "In a few
days' time, we'll see how much *she* likes
being cast adrift, eating nothing but
barnacles and drinking—"

"Don't think about it, sir," Sham
soothed. His boss got a bit crazy
whenever he talked about his recent
troubles at the hands of Scarlet Silver and
her crew.

Gilbert Gauntlet calmed down. He

pulled a large stick out of an inner
pocket and tapped it on his hand. "Time
for a little bish-bash-bosh," he said,
striding for the cabin steps. "What fun."

"Your tongue's like smelly sandpaper,
Ralph," Scarlet mumbled, pushing the
ship's cat off her face the following
morning. "Go and find a haddock to lick,
will you?"

Yawning, she rubbed her eyes and
gazed across the pale blue water to where
55 Ocean Drive rocked gently in the dawn
current.

"Two more days till we find that
treasure," said Grandpa Jack jubilantly,
rinsing his socks in the sea and wringing
them out before pulling them back on to
his feet.

"Assumin' them letters on the compass don't mean diddly-piddly," One-Eyed Scott added.

Scarlet was sure the letters were important. She just really, really hoped she'd understand them when the time was right.

"All aboard!" she called, dragging Cedric away from the enormous sandcastle he'd gone straight back to building as soon as he'd woken up.

Lila gave herself a final brisk rub with her homemade sand-and-ash exfoliator, polished her glasses and knotted her hankie firmly on her head. Melvin twisted his moustache upwards into a smiley shape as Ralph clambered on to his head. One-Eyed Scott tossed the remains of the grilled octopus up to a flock of screeching gulls, who snapped it out of the air like it was candyfloss, knocking both Bluebeard and Lipstick out of the way. Then everyone waded back to the ship.

Melvin hauled up the anchor and Scarlet took the helm. Soon the wind was flooding the sails, tugging *55 Ocean Drive* along like a balloon in a gale.

"This is all right, isn't it?" said Cedric as they scudded through the day. "The bedsheets are dry already, and Dad only put them out this morning."

A calm night followed. The stars glowed and flashed overhead like disco lights, and Grandpa Jack sat happily at the prow with the largest night-fishing rod in his collection. But the next morning, everything changed.

First, the sun disappeared. A heavy mist appeared from nowhere, wrapping *55 Ocean Drive* in a blanket of white cotton wool. An eerie quiet descended.

"I don't like this," said One-Eyed Scott, helping Scarlet at the wheel. "It gives me the creeps."

The mist was already so thick that Scarlet could hardly see the sides of the ship. "We steered through that fog OK last time," she said, trying to sound confident. "What's so different about this?"

The old pirate shook his head, clattering his chicken bones. "I don't like it," he repeated.

A roaring sound drifted towards them. Straining her eyes through the whiteness, Scarlet tried to see what was making the noise. She lost her grip on the wheel as it

jerked out of her hands. One-Eyed Scott
tried to catch it, but it spun away and
out of control.

They felt the ship starting to turn.

Cedric's voice floated down through the mist from the crow's nest.

"Scarlet?"

"Yes?" Scarlet called, staring at the whizzing ship's wheel and trying not to feel completely fudge-brained with fear. The boat was turning … faster …

"There's a swirly-shaped spinning thingy in the water up ahead of us. I think we're heading right for the middle of it. What do you call it …?"

"A whirlpool?" Scarlet said.

"Yeah," Cedric told her. "One of them. What should we do?"

The answer came to Scarlet like a bullet. The swirly shape at the heart of the map's compass. The letters …

"L … E … A … N!" she yelled, grabbing

One-Eyed Scott and towing him to the
ship's rail. "OUR LIVES DEPEND ON IT!
LEAN!!"

Tremendous Treasure

The roar from the whirlpool was
deafening. The current sucked at the
ship's keel. Everything was sliding
sideways. One-Eyed Scott and Grandpa
Jack's Fishomatic flying-fish fishing
machine bounced off the deck and
disappeared into the churning water.

"Climb on each other's shoulders!"
Scarlet shouted, as Cedric whizzed down
from the crow's nest like a monkey with

a swarm of wasps on its tail. "There isn't much time!"

Bluebeard and Lipstick squawked and screeched as everyone scrambled on top of each other. Melvin had been an acrobat in a former life, and shouted instructions. Feet slid over chins and noses and trod on fingers and toes.

55 Ocean Drive was now tilting so far that the sails were almost touching the raging water. So, on the opposite side of the ship:

Ralph sat on Cedric,
  who balanced on Scarlet,
  who clung to Grandpa Jack,
  who sat on One-Eyed Scott
  (who swore a lot),
    who grabbed tightly on to Lila,
    who locked herself around
      Melvin's neck.

Melvin
braced himself
and leaned
backwards. The tottering
tower of pirates leaned with
him. Ralph wrapped his tail
tightly over Cedric's screwed-up
eyes. And unbelievably – blessedly –
the ship began to pull out of its spin
and drift away from the whirling torrent.

The mist cleared. The tower of pirates
collapsed in a heap on the deck as the
ship righted herself. They had made it.

Scarlet wriggled out from underneath
Cedric and Ralph. She heard a groaning

sound under her feet. There was a dull
SNAP.

"What was that?" said One-Eyed Scott,
untangling his chicken bones from where
they'd looped themselves around Lila's
mist-spattered glasses.

"Sounds like a damaged strut in the
hull," said Grandpa Jack.

"Yes?" said Lila brightly.

"Grandpa means the
bottom of the boat is
broken," Cedric
translated.

Lila looked alarmed. "The bottom of the boat? Boats with broken bottoms usually sink."

"It'll be a little bit of timber damage," said Scarlet soothingly. "It'll take more than a measly whirlpool to sink *55 Ocean Drive*. We'll be fine, so long as we don't hear any water rushing around below deck anytime soon."

WHOOOOOOOOOOOOOSH.

Melvin cocked his head. "Did someone leave the bath running?" he said.

55 Ocean Drive started tipping like a three-legged chair. Scarlet ran for the cabin door and flung it open. She stared at the water flooding up the stairs. She couldn't believe what she was seeing. *55 Ocean Drive* was well and truly scuppered.

Scarlet's heart felt like it was breaking.

Her pirate ship – her home – her first pirate voyage. Everything was over.

She took a deep, captainly breath.

"ABANDON SHIP!" she shouted. "WE'RE GOING DOWN!"

"My shoes!" Lila moaned.

"My cactus collection!" groaned Melvin.

"MY EGGBOX ROCKET!" Cedric roared.

"We can't get any of them," Scarlet said, pulling her family away from the stricken cabin steps. "Where's the dinghy gone?"

"The whirlpool got it," said One-Eyed Scott, staring at the frayed ropes where the ship's dinghy should still have been attached to the ship.

55 Ocean Drive groaned like an injured animal. It tipped further sideways. The stern was already sinking below the surface of the water.

"Right," said Scarlet, trying to control her racing heartbeat. "We have to swim for it, or we'll drown."

"We can't!" said Grandpa Jack in a trembly voice. "Out there – look. Them large, pink things with feelers on their heads. Ain't they ...?"

Everyone goggled at the water. Scarlet felt her legs go numb with terror.

"Oh ..." Melvin gasped, twisting his fingers so tightly into his moustache that he couldn't pull them out again.

"Crunchin' crocodiles," One-Eyed Scott whispered. "The doom of Long Joan Silver awaits us all."

A school of giant shrimp had poked their heads out of the waves. The seawater sloshed over the lower half of their scaly pink bodies, making them look like they were wearing purple trousers. They stared at the rapidly sinking *55 Ocean Drive* and waggled the long feelers on their heads.

Scarlet forced her frozen brain into action.

If they stayed aboard, they were fish food. If they jumped, they were fish food. But at least they were fish food that was trying to survive.

"JUMP!" she roared. "AND THAT'S AN ORDER!"

"Oh bottoms, oh bottoms, oh bottoms," moaned Bluebeard, darting after Lipstick like a terrified blue and yellow arrow. The crew plunged overboard. Even Ralph struck out on his own, with Melvin paddling madly behind him. Grandpa Jack and One-Eyed Scott whacked the water with their arms and roared pirate curses at the shrimp in case they could somehow scare them off. Cedric activated the flipper attachments on his leg splints and grabbed Scarlet with one arm and Lila with the other. The flippers churned

up the water so much that Scarlet
couldn't see a thing.

*Perhaps it's better not to watch a giant
shrimp as it bites into you,* she thought
dimly as she floundered around.

Through the spray and the forest of shrimpy feelers surrounding them, Scarlet saw a stretch of pale sand creep into the corner of her eye.

"That way!" she choked, spitting out a mouthful of seawater and pointing.

They struck, flailed, splashed and kicked. Scarlet even caught the scaly side of a shrimp with the pointy toe of her red satin pirate boots, and heard a shrimpy "OOF!"

"Land," Scarlet croaked, feeling her feet touch down on solid ground. "Lovely, lumpy, sandy *land* ..."

Grandpa Jack and One-Eyed Scott sloshed ashore, waved their fists at the circling shrimp. Cedric was pulling off his flipper attachments and flopping down on the sand. Lila and Melvin were kissing. Ralph was eating a fish that he'd somehow had time to catch whilst swimming for his life.

"Yuck," said Bluebeard, fluttering down and landing on Scarlet's shoulder in a ball of soggy feathers as Lipstick looped joyfully through the air.

Scarlet stroked her budgie, feeling her heartbeat slowly settling back to normal. The remains of *55 Ocean Drive* had washed closer to the sandbank, hitting shallow waters. Now it was only half-submerged, but still broken and wet. *Perhaps we can patch her up again and sail on …* Scarlet thought, hope fluttering feebly inside her. *If only the stinking shrimp would go away …*

She turned away from the sea and stared. Up ahead, their sandy patch of land melted into a shallow turquoise lagoon. The lagoon stretched towards an island whose mountains were peeping through the mist like shy green giants. The distant song of exotic birds and the rustle of palm trees floated towards the bedraggled pirates.

"Is that what I think it is?" Lila gasped.

Scarlet pulled the Vague Vagabond's pendant from around her neck and looked at it. She stared back across the lagoon.

The shape of the mountains matched exactly.

Feeling like she was in a dream, Scarlet stepped into the lagoon and began to wade through the pale, warm water. Rainbow-coloured fish darted around her feet. She could hear the others wading

behind her, chatting and laughing.

"... showed them murdering molluscs what-for, eh Scotty? Joan would've been proud ..."

"... the birds, Melvin – listen ..."

"... Bottoms ..."

"... not *that* bird, dear ..."

Scarlet waded on, her eyes fixed on the island before her.

" … don't do your flippers, Cedric love – you'll scare the fish …"

" … I'll scare them into a fish pie, eh Grandpa? Ha ha!"

Scarlet was the only one who saw the lone figure standing on the shoreline ahead. Her head started spinning.

" … course, I knowed them letters spelt something only I was workin' on *Neal* and I don't know nobody called Neal …"

The long purple velvet frock coat. The thigh-length black boots. Long grey hair whipping around in the breeze.

"For goodness *sake* Ralph, will you leave those fish alone …"

The water was now at ankle level. The chatter died away. Ralph swallowed a small wave as Lila screamed and Grandpa Jack clutched at his beard.

"Hello, treasures," said Long Joan
Silver, reaching out her arms to hold her
family tight.

EPILOGUE

The End ...?

"You thought the *shrimp* got me?" Long
Joan Silver threw back her head and
roared with laughter. "Them pink fellas
don't have a tooth in their plug-ugly
heads! What was they going to do, suck
me to death?"

"Don't joke, Gran," Scarlet begged. Her
arms were wrapped tightly around her
grandmother's neck, in case Long Joan
disappeared and the whole wonderful,

glorious last ten minutes had been one of those dreams you never want to end. "That's what the crew said."

"You was eaten," Grandpa Jack said, still staring at his wife like he'd seen a ghost. "I *seed* you get eaten, love. Honest I did. Otherwise I'd have jumped in and rescued you."

Long Joan patted Grandpa Jack's hand. "Of course you would've, Jack my duck. And I *was* eaten. Only I got spat out again."

"Like Lipstick," said Cedric.

"That's it, lad," said Long Joan.

"Corn-fed codfish and crinkly candyfloss," said One-Eyed Scott. "You is the queen of pirates, Joanie."

Lila burst into tears for the fourth time in as many minutes and buried her head in Melvin's extremely soggy neck.

Scarlet looked up at her grandmother. "So are *you* the Vague Vagabond, Gran?" she asked.

Long Joan Silver cocked her head, almost knocking Lipstick off his perch on her hat. "I s'pose I am now," she said. "The *old* Vague Vagabond – a dear he was, fell completely in love with me ..."

" ... course he did, Joanie," said Grandpa Jack, stroking Long Joan's hair. "They always do."

"Don't they?" Long Joan said fondly. "Anyways, the old fella passed on to the happy treasure trove in the sky some time back, leaving me alone on his island. So's if anyone comes lookin' for the Vague Vagabond and his treasure – like I did all them years back, leaving you that pendant and all them clues across the Seven Seas in case I never made it back – they'll find me instead. Not that they will, of course," she added with a touch of pride in her voice. "Only a family like the Silvers was ever going to work out them riddles and make it here in one piece."

"Is that why you made it so complicated?" Scarlet asked.

"That's it, treasure," Long Joan said. "The number of villains out there as'd sell their mothers to find this place – you wouldn't believe it."

Scarlet thought of Gilbert Gauntlet. She glanced back at her family and knew they were all thinking of him too. "We do believe it, Gran," she said.

"Nice island, this, by the way," Long Joan said, waving her arms at the fragrant flowers and shady trees that lined the white beach. "Plenty of bananas, great seafood. Only thing missing was my family. And now you're here. Perfect."

"Only just," said Melvin. "We had a few problems."

"Ah, but that's all part of it, see?" Long Joan said with a slow, gold-toothed grin. "You wasn't going to be much use to me if you'd come along like a bunch of telly-

watching townies. You're proper pirates
now – and right good 'uns too, by the
looks of you."

Scarlet was still fizzing with questions.
But suddenly everything fell into place.
"Of course," she gasped. "It's *you*, Gran.
You're the tremendous treasure!"

The Silvers and One-Eyed Scott went
wild. They whooped and flung their arms
around the most famous lady pirate on
the Seven Seas. Long Joan Silver was a

treasure all right – a treasure they never wanted to lose again.

Lila gave a watery smile. "I can't think of anything else I'd rather have found," she said, and burst into tears again.

"Except maybe some gold," Cedric said.

"Cedric!" Melvin gasped, squeezing Ralph so hard that the cat shot out of his hands like a wet bar of soap and almost caught Bluebeard in mid-air.

"I'm only *saying*," Cedric protested. "We're pirates, aren't we? And we look for treasure, don't we? It's brilliant to see you, Granny – you're seriously cool and everything. But … I kind of thought we'd find maybe a bit of actual treasure. You know?"

"Spoke like a proper pirate, Cedric lad," Long Joan said. She twinkled at her family again. "So that brings me to the nub of it. It's nice you thinking this whole hunt's bin about me. But that ain't quite so. There's a *real* treasure – a proper one, not this flesh and blood one you're gettin' all soppy about, " she added, thumbing her chest. "The old fella told me about it. Well, he hinted – Vague by name, vague by nature, he was. Onlys I couldn't go and find it on my own, with no boat and no crew. Now that's all changed. I've gotten me an unstoppable team. It's time to go on a *real* treasure hunt, my treasures – as a proper family at last!"

Wet and shivering, Gilbert Gauntlet peered out from behind a palm tree. Despite everything, he – *Gilbert Gauntlet* –

had found the Vague Vagabond's island. Following the girly had worked. She'd been too busy cuddling the old lady to notice him crawling out of the lagoon. And her crew were as useless as lamb chops in a piranha pool. He may have lost half his businesses, his son, his yacht, his raft and henchman down that whirlpool, half his buttons and the feather in his hat. *But he was still here.* He had to admire himself for that.

He watched as the girly and her family cavorted around the sand like they had termites in their trousers. It was comical.

"Treasure, eh?" he muttered, clutching the trunk of the palm tree and giggling in a way that he dimly realised sounded a bit mad. "I'm right behind you, girly. All the way …"

HB 978 0 340 98912 8
PB 978 0 340 95967 1

HB 978 0 340 98913 5
PB 978 0 340 95968 8

HB 978 0 340 98914 2
PB 978 0 340 95969 5

HB 978 0 340 98915 9
PB 978 0 340 95970 1

HB 978 0 340 98916 6
PB 978 0 340 95971 8

Read more of Scarlet Silver's adventures on the High Seas